Confessions of the Ageing Swimmers

by

Nick Owen

Illustrations by Paul Warren

Published by Nick Owen Publishing, Lincoln, UK.

Nick Owen Publishing Ltd is registered in England and Wales as a Company Limited by Guarantee (09435925)

Email   nick@nickowenpublishing.co.uk
Web   www.nickowenpublishing.co.uk
ISBN   9798345124703

Thanks to Alexander Moore for his essential manuscript editing expertise.

A catalogue record for this book is available from the British Library.

First published November 2024

NOP

Preface

What would you do if you heard someone confess to the most heinous moral crime but there was nothing you could do about it?

Hardly a day goes by without someone telling us off about our bodies: they're too big, too small, in the wrong place at the wrong time, or they just don't behave in the way we want them to.

How we interact with contemporary sport can be a productive way to explore our relationship with our bodies and how they respond to the demands we make of them. We follow performers and athletes, clubs and countries, the ups and downs of the elite; and we are encouraged – daily – to get off our sofas and run that elusive marathon, to join in and be part of some team or another. We identify, and sometimes, over-identify with our sporting heroes. We become appalled at their behaviour when they fall from grace, but can't help getting drawn into their stories, whatever age we are, and whatever age they are.

The *Confessions* series of books explore these matters in, hopefully, an entertaining and thought-provoking manner. Whilst a particular sport might be more prominent, the books themselves are not really about that sport at all. *Tennis Player* explored dreams and delusions; *Footballer*, loneliness; *Basketball Player* was my take on the COVID-19 pandemic, *Figure Skater* explored the expectations of growing up and adulthood.

Swimmers follows in this tradition through relating the trials and tribulations of 18-year-old Leo. A Generation Z-er who's already been on the receiving end of too much *sturm und drang* in his life so far: the COVID-19 pandemic has left its mark on his confidence, the behaviour of recent governments has left him despairing of any political change, ever, anywhere and the "Climate Crisis" has rattled his belief in the future of the planet. Things aren't looking too bright for Leo, apart from the opportunity to become a trainee lifeguard at his local swimming pool (their motto: "*Building a Better You. A Better Family. A Better Britain*"). Employed on a six-month, national minimum wage contract, Leo doesn't have much time to make a lasting impression. He struggles with the demands made by his employer for the first five months and is constantly fending off the desire to sleep, eat, party, do the right thing with the right people and then sleep again. The classic round peg in a square hole. The demands of the "World of Work" aren't quite what Leo imagined they would be, and he struggles to meet the demands his employer makes of him and the other young people in their care.

His potential future employment at the *Day One Leisure Centre* is looking precarious in his last month until a sudden, shocking event in one of the pool's changing cubicles gives him a glimpse of a potential future for himself: not just as a lifeguard, but as the saviour of the souls of sinners. Inspired by events and overheard conversations in some of Nottingham's finest swimming pools – as well as some of the oldest Biblical myths – *Swimmers* aims to give you an entertaining insight into just why there are more swimming pools than churches these days.

Part Two of Swimmers is composed of a seven-part poem called *Christmas Shopping*, suitable we thought given that the end of Swimmers takes place the night before Christmas in (spoiler alert) what's left of the swimming pool and its community of swimmers and sinners.

I conceived *Christmas Shopping* originally as a "Scattered Poem": four stanzas, three of which I "scattered" to three different audiences, the fourth part remaining with myself. Audiences were invited to complete the poem, by contacting the three other audiences, combining their three respective parts and then returning the partially completed poem to me. I then added the fourth and final verse and the completed, intact poem was sent to all of the audience members. So far, so good: I tried it many times over with many different audience sets but it seemed the task was too much and I didn't get a single response from anyone. No matter: Christmas is a mad, busy time, and obviously the last thing anyone wanted to do was collect bits of a scattered poem and go to the trouble of recombining it!

After this abortive attempt at bringing people together at Christmas time, I developed the central four stanza poem with six ancillary characters (all animals of some description) who play a minor if not negligible role in the main *Christmas Shopping* poem. It was my take on a Christmas Nativity scene, albeit through the lens of improbable attendees at a secular Christmas Eve happening.

This final poem is presented here and could be envisaged as a seven panel polyptych which may eventually be transformed into a large stained-glass window. Paul Warren, our illustrator-in-residence, and

4

myself are already talking through those options and may be able to shed some light on their outcome sometime in 2025.

In the meantime, here's to all your future Happy Christmases!

IN THE BEGINNING…

1. The Hole in the Space Time Fabric

"Fuck it." I just couldn't help myself. One minute I'm swabbing down the floor of a cubicle in the mixed changing area by the side of the municipal swimming pool; the next I notice a small change in paint colour of the wall adjacent to the next cubicle. It's about the size of a one penny piece and, if you're sat down on the cubicle bench, is roughly at head height. Normally, you wouldn't be able to tell there was anything untoward about this cubicle; but today, there's something about the light, the atmosphere in the pool, and the lack of swimmers getting changed. So, I lingered a bit longer than normal with my cubicle cleaning and detected this small ripple in the usual steady state reality of the municipal swimming pool's mixed changing rooms.

I should have left there and then (and sometimes wish I had done). I should have blinked, turned a blind eye – and my back – on this glitch in my time space continuum and continued with my cleaning. It would have made life a whole lot easier for everyone. But no, of course I didn't! I looked closer and found that the slight colour change was due to a small plug of dense cotton wool inserted into a hole in the wall. And, little by little, it was possible to pull out that fabric plug to reveal a small aperture: and then, if you were to place your eye against it, you could squint through into the adjacent cubicle.

Startled, I put it back in a bit of a rush, but it's obvious now that the wall has been tampered with. The disturbed fabric plug reveals the lie; the partition is not intact, it is no longer a coherent and safe barrier between this cubicle and its neighbour. I try to flatten it, smooth out the plug to make it flush with the wall, but I'm only making the situation worse. I wonder if I should tell my boss, Petr, but then think better of that and stop myself. I don't know why, but something tells me that he won't be happy with me finding it, that he'll find some way of implicating me in the construction of this peep hole (because that's clearly what it is), and that somehow, I'll be responsible for someone else's misdemeanour. And since I've only got another month to go before I know whether I've passed my probation period and can secure a job as lifeguard for the rest of my life, it's not something I want to risk.

I end up botching the botch-job and panic momentarily. I've gotta get out of here, away from the cubicle, the pool, the gym, the car park.

I'll have to erase my time sheet to make sure no one can see that I was on duty on or around the time the peep hole was discovered.

But it's pointless. (I'm soon arguing with myself again.) Too many people know I'm here.

"Fuck it." Petr has already given me a cursory nod when I logged in earlier; Monica had studiously ignored me as per usual; I had had a couple of laughs over the state of the showers with Gerbil, the café owner, who had once again tried flogging me some healthy breakfast on our break. So, there's no way ever that I'm going to be able to prove to anyone that I was nowhere near the swimming pool's changing area when the peep hole was discovered. So, I do what any self-respecting swimming pool attendant would do in time of panic: go and act the role of the lifeguard. I clambered up the ladder to the top seat and perched there, ready for a call to action. Happily, we've never had a call to action in the whole five months that I've been at our pool, but you can never be too safe and as Petr never tires of telling us, "Lifeguards have to be eternally vigilant."

Eternally?

I find myself arguing with myself every time he says it. That's a mighty long time. But it's what I need now – well, long enough to forget the peep hole at any rate.

2. The Serpents

"When are you going to get down off your throne, Mufasa?" A voice hurtled into my consciousness from the darkest recesses of the universe of my mind, and I woke with a start. Petr was leaning on the lifeguard's chair and staring up at me from the poolside. I'd dozed off; the deepest felony a swimming pool lifeguard would not dare to even dream of committing. As well as startling me, Petr knew how to irritate me and he took every opportunity he could, on account of my name: Leo.

"Leo the Lion?" he had asked of me quizzically on the first shift of my first day at the pool all those months ago.

"No, just Leo. It's short for Leopold. On account of my dad's family."

"Oh, so you have a father then?" he asked, raising his eyebrows to achieve maximum performance effect for the benefit of the other attendants who had also started that day. A couple of the girls giggled but stopped when he turned his stare on them. "And what are your lovely names, you lovely girls?"

"Beatrice," mumbled one.

"Anastasia," bellowed the other.

Petr looked delighted. "Anastasia, Beatrice and Leopold. What splendid names for such splendid young people. Such breeding, obviously. Such class. Well, you won't find much class in this neck of the woods, will they, pet?" He turned to his side kick, Monica, who hadn't taken her gaze off him the moment he had started our induction. As his assistant, Monica clearly felt at home in the pool and knew her place in the pecking order.

"None whatsoever Petr," she purred, "quite the contrary, knowing what our swimmers are like."

"So, first off, we'll have to acquaint you with our working methods and our terms of address. In future you'll be known as Beat, Anna and Leo. It'll save on our breathing– vital in a swimming pool when you never know when you'll need every last gasp, on account of having to rescue some errant swimmer who's struggling in the shallow end."

Beatrice made to interject Petr but it was no use, he was in full flow.

"Don't interrupt, Beat. I'm about to impart the most important knowledge you'll need to get you through these early days here at the glorious Day One Municipal Swimming Pool, at the heart of the community as we like to say, don't we pet?"

"That's right, Petr," affirmed Monica, looking at him longingly.

"But..." Beatrice tried again.

"And don't interrupt Petr," Monica added sharply, for once turning her attention to the errant new attendant. "you'll need to understand everything he's about to tell you. It could be a matter of life and death when you least expect it. So pay full attention!"

Beatrice blinked and shut her mouth. Monica was clearly one not to be trifled with, least of all poolside.

"Thank you pet," Petr picked up where he left off. "In the hearts, minds and spirits of our community. That's where we make our mark and that's why you're all interested in a job here isn't it?" There was a protracted silence amongst us trainees. "I said, isn't it?" Petr tried again, this time with a detectable menace in his voice.

"Yes, Petr... er... I suppose so," we managed between us, not the most convincing trainees it has to be said.

"Now I know they're not the best paid positions in the world..." He stopped to stare that Petr stare at Anastasia who had stifled a guffaw. She continued to stifle it, at some obvious discomfort to herself. "But they will be, after all your training, and after you have successfully passed your probationary period, proper jobs which will see you being paid regularly in return for your time and commitment to service. And that is what we are all about, always, every minute of every day. What are we about, pet?"

"Service, Petr." Monica duly obliged, "Service with a capital 'S'" she hissed, holding the final syllable before letting it fade.

The induction plodded along and we three were thankful when Petr had run out of words and it ground to a stop. He sent us back to the reception area, and so, our long-awaited careers in guarding lives had begun.

"So, what do you think you're doing up there, Mufasa? The pool closed ten minutes ago." It was a rude awakening, forcing me to suddenly fast-forward five months back to the present. He was right. I'd dozed off and missed the final bell which summoned everyone from the pool and back to the showers and changing room.

"Oh... sorry, Petr. I just drifted off. It's been a long shift."

He looked at me in disbelief.

"You've only been here for three hours. Let's face it, you've been asleep on the job ever since you got here however many months ago that was. If I've told you once, I've told you countless times. You.

Don't. Sleep. On. Watch!" and with every word, he gave the lifeguard's chair a good shake.

"Yes, Petr, sorry, Petr." I jumped off the chair before he managed to dislodge me into the pool and started walking to the staff room.

"Where do you think you're going? You can mop down now. And don't hang around. The next lot will be here in an hour."

"But…" It was pointless to protest. So, I turned around and instead headed towards the cubicles, partly in dread, partly intrigued. ☐

3. The Gen Zee Call to Action

I stood at the entrance to the changing rooms, hesitating, before walking around the corner and facing the two connected cubicles: one on the left and one on the right. I look at the cubicle on the right – my cubicle. It's funny how the cubicle has become mine. Its door is shut.

Do I go in or not?

I walked nervously towards the door. Fortunately, there was nobody around so I gave the door a gentle push and was amazed to see nothing on the wall. There was no sign of a plug of cotton wool, no sign of any carpentry on new plaster work. The wall is seamless. I can't believe it. I walked in, stroked my hand on the wall where I thought the peep hole was, to find nothing. Someone, something, has repaired the wall. Completely confused, I sat down on the bench and lay my head at where I thought the hole was. Nothing, no sign of any disturbance whatsoever.

There are footsteps outside. I sit up with a start as the door's pushed wide open.

"Are you still here?" asks Petr savagely. "I told you to get onto your next shift."

"Sorry Petr," I replied. "I just got overwhelmed with tiredness. I had to sit down."

"Well stand back up again. Get out the front and get on with your job. Been here five months and you still don't get it do you? You'll really have to lift your game my lad if you stand any chance at all of passing your probation period. Right now, I don't give you much of a chance. And quite frankly, the sooner the next month passes, the happier I shall be to get shot of you. You Gen Zee-ers or whatever it is you call yourselves these days. You don't know you're born. You think you're born with all the rights in the world and none of the responsibilities. You think you can just dial in whenever it suits you..." His rant echoed around the changing rooms, becoming ever fainter as he disappeared towards the reception.

Nightmare. My head dropped and I slid meekly out to the reception. The usual tasks: check the registers for the next intake of swimmers, tick off the health and safety equipment, stare at the fire alarm, wonder about the defibrillator, make sure the floors are dry, confirm with Gerbil that he's opening the café. But underneath the scrutiny and the ticking of the boxes, I'm puzzled. Nonplussed.

Did I just imagine that small cotton wool wad in the wall?

4. The Customer is Always, *Always* Right

"Day One Leisure Centre, can I help you? That's right sir. Yes, sir. Sorry to hear that sir. Ok. Yes. No. Yes. No. I'm sure… No, I'm sorry, I didn't mean to interrupt you. I am listening. I really am…"

I'm scheduled on reception this afternoon which usually involves dealing with calls from irate centre members who have been disgruntled by something earlier that day for which we are equally invariably responsible for. Except that often we're not. But Petr insists that the customer is always, *always*, right; any suggestion that this might not be true in every instance, will attract the wrath of Monica. The idea that you might challenge the veracity of what the customer is telling you, that it might be flawed in some way, is one thing; but to challenge the Word of Petr is quite another. In her eyes, it is an offence punishable by regular and repeated humiliation whenever the opportunity arises.

This particular member continues to drone on and on in his spirit of self-rectitude, uttering all kinds of impossibilities and contradictions about the showers, the hair dryers, the state of the floors and why have we stolen his swimming cap? I eventually recognise who it is: it's the member we call Oliver, or the Turtle, on account of his swimming style, which has an uncanny resemblance to the Olive Ridley species of the sea turtle. The benefit of this naming is that if me and the girls happen to be dissing him poolside and he's in the proximity, he won't necessarily know who we're talking about. And it's very easy to take to dissing Oliver given his unending ability to complain.

His complaints are frequently about events which in any normal universe would be impossible. He swears to God he was at last night's lane swimming session. Impossible, we were shut for yet more maintenance. He insists the sandwich he was sold in the café contained white bread. Impossible, Gerbil only sells wholesome granary bread sandwiches which accounts for why the café is about to go bust. But truth and veracity obviously mean nothing to Oliver, and he continues with his tale of woes, gradually shifting from chastising me, the girls, the management to the resident flock of seagulls in the car park for every little transgression he has had the misfortune to suffer over the last week. I find it difficult not to doze off while listening to this tirade until he utters the unforgettable words:

"And as for that peephole in cubicle two. Words fail me. I am disgusted…"

He finally runs out of words and I wake with a start to see Petr staring at me.

"What's up?" he asks. "Cat tongue?"

I'm shocked and unsure what to say or do next. Oliver hangs up and I'm left with the single dial tone playing out into the empty reception area.

5. Flotsam and Jetsam

"Poolside. Now." Petr shakes me from my Oliver-induced reverie, who I now realise shares the same secret with me: the spotting of the peephole. I nod, and head back to the pool via the changing area but this time avoid the offending corridor and cubicle two. I station myself on the lifeguard seat and look out into the pool.

Two slow old women, whom we have nicknamed "Flotsam" and "Jetsam", are back in today, making their excruciating way up the slow lane. One slow stroke after another, accompanied by their constant chatting which characterises their hour in the pool. It's a veritable soundtrack which, because today's session is so quiet, can be heard not only in the slow lane but by the occupant of the lifeguard's seat, which in today's case happens to be me. I would much rather clean Petr's trainers with my tongue than listen to their rambling as they slowly drift up and down the lanes. Unnervingly, they also have the habit of finishing each other's sentences, this means that if you shut your eyes, you can't be too sure which of them said what.

"A pound of mince. Five pounds of onions. Two pounds of tripe. Leg of lamb. Big bag of spuds." I can make out Flotsam splashing her way towards the deep end.

"Ooh lovely. Nothing better than a–" begins Jetsam.

"–roast leg of lamb on a Sunday." Flotsam finishes for her. "We're doing it different this week: the fam's coming over on Saturday."

"Really? What's the–"

"–big occasion? Fred's going to motorcross Sunday. First time–"

"–in years. Aren't you worried?"

"What can I do?"

"I say. Roast leg of lamb on a Saturday. Doesn't seem right."

"I told him, that's the last time, we're not doing that again. All the–"

"–disruption. All the cleaning up. And what are you going to do–"

"–on Sunday when he's off on his trick cyclist stuff? No idea."

"Never mind duck. Back to normal next week."

"I'm not so sure."

"Really?"

"Trick cycling is one thing. But motorcross? Where will it lead, Viv, that's what I want to know, where will it lead? No good, I'll be bound."

"Are you ready to–"

"–get out? Two more lengths."

"Ok, after you."

"Mustn't forget–"

"–the mint sauce. I do love a roast leg of lamb on a Sunday."

And so they continue, heading slowly up the lane, their chatter finally being drowned by the swell of the hubbub of the other swimmers who've joined the session. I must say I'm grateful when it gets busy; all that over-hearing other people's conversations is just plain wrong.

6. Sealife

Rudolph is wizened little man who must be at least 90 as far as I can tell. He creaks himself down into the pool and his body folds itself in half almost automatically, like a book is being closed. But he's clearly not ready to have his story finished just yet, so he slowly stretches back out, steps gingerly through the water until he can stand up no more and with the water lapping at his ears, he pushes out tentatively to start his breaststroke, and miraculously, he floats and makes unsteady progress through the water.

As he's in the very slow lane, he's met by some buffeting wash from the centre of the pool which he navigates through, but I hold my breath sometimes when the water washes over him and it looks for a moment like he's drowning. But no, a few seconds later he's resurfaced and continues his journey, unperturbed and looking even more like a drowned rat than he did before.

"Morning, ladies!" he calls out to Flotsam and Jetsam. They ignore him and continue their weekend planning.

"Nothing better than a roast leg of lamb on a Sunday."

"We're doing it different this week: the fam's coming over on Saturday."

"I say. Roast leg of lamb on a Saturday. Doesn't seem right."

"Have a great morning!" he'll manage to call out to Bartok, one of the slightly quicker swimmers in the adjacent lane, as he continues towards the safety of the shallow end.

"Never mind the day! Have a great time! All the time!" responds Bartok, his big Irish friend in a white swimming cap as he reaches poolside and tries to affect a seamless underwater turn. Except it's not seamless and he splutters and splashes as his timing gets the worse of him and he must resort to clutching at Rudolph who somehow stands his ground and helps his friend from suffering the indignity of drowning in the shallow end.

"Thank you, Rudolph."

"At your service."

"I think that's enough for the time being."

"Yes, no point over doing it. Good morning, young lady!" Rudolph spots a young woman in a yellow swimsuit jump into the shallow end a few lanes away, gather herself together, and set off under water at pace towards the deep end. She flips up her legs as if to acknowledge his greeting but is incapable of saying any more due to the fact that she spends an inordinate amount of time under water. "How on earth does she do that?" he muses.

"No idea," responds Bartok who proceeds to haul his massive frame up the poolside ladder and stumble back to the changing rooms. "Must be related to a mermaid." He's very unsteady on his feet so I follow him just to make sure he's okay. I also think this would be a good chance to check out cubicle two and see that there's no untoward peephole activity going on. Just for a couple of moments, mind, no longer. Just enough to check. No more. So, with Bartok safely standing in the shower, I head off to cubicles one and two.

Quickly looking around to check the coast is clear, I step into cubicle two, shut the door, sit on the bench and look at the space where the peephole had been.

Nothing there. I sigh, relieved, although I'm not sure why. I rest my head on the wall and briefly shut my eyes. I must have been imagining it. Thank God I didn't tell Petr. It would have been the end of me. The ridicule would have been unbearable. I soon become aware of some scuffling in cubicle one. The partition isn't thick enough to stop noise spillage and, unwittingly and unwillingly, I found myself listening to the activities from the other side. I can tell by the breathing and gasping that it's Rudolph. He's clearly had enough exercise in the pool and I'm about to call out to him to see if he's ok when I hear him whisper,

"I really must stop looking up women's legs when they swim past."

I hold my breath like I've gone deep sea diving with our resident mermaid, and try to stop my pulse racing, my heart beating and my ears from hearing anything else. Anything to ensure that my presence isn't detected, that I am invisible. I wish I could die on the spot or, even better, be teleported to some distant galaxy. But this is not a service that the Day One Municipal Leisure offers anyone, least of all its trainee lifeguards who have another twenty-nine days to go before their career is confirmed or terminated.

7. Have a great time! All the time!

One advantage of working through an interminable probation period is that you get to hear from swimmers from all sorts of swims of life. Some of these swimmers have formed very definite opinions of the world as they know it and are only too happy to communicate those opinions to us lesser mortals who are just a modest fraction of their age. Bartok was a case in point and the day after I'd inadvertently overheard Rudolph's transgression, he decided to share with me his fully informed opinion about the value of leisure centres.

"They say that more people go to gyms these days than they do churches, and I can quite see why. There's no swimming pools in churches, no opportunities to hang around in the gym talking to your mates, no way you're going to be able to get on a treadmill and step your heart out to the banging tunes that fill the air of the communion of gymnasts that gather, come what may. I don't see the attraction of churches at all. I mean, who wouldn't want to count their heart rate, work out on a regime which promotes fat loss, muscle building, steps, cardiac strength. No way you can do that at church. Just this morning I had tracked my lap length and found that I had got it down to under six minutes per one hundred metres and I was really pleased with myself. All those sessions in the e-gym have really paid off, and I'm managing to keep my calories deficit on the negative side too, so what's not to like?"

Bartok could be a bit of a bore sometimes about his health. Not least when he was pontificating in the shallow end to his friend Rudolph who could hardly get a word in. Not surprising really as he had clearly worn himself out on that last twenty-five metres and had just struggled in to reach poolside. I swear though that instead of listening to his big Irish friend that every now and then cast furtive glances to the women swimmers in the next lane who had just effortlessly turned on their heads at the edge of the pool, and continued their morning swim back towards the deep end, not missing a stroke, and without being distracted by the pontiff in the slow lane.

"They also say that it's not exercise that loses you weight, but that it's much more about your diet and I have to say I have to disagree, Rudolph. I've started tracking my calorie intake in recent days to see if there is a correlation between my active energy usage, my dietary sins, my weight and of course my BMI and I have to say that my evidence points to activity being far more of a determining factor when it comes to weight loss than diet. Either that or six pints of Guinness every night are better for you than any dietician would have you believe." At this, he guffawed a loud, Irish belly laugh which sent ripples down and across the pool, almost knocking Rudolph off balance.

"Quite so," Rudolph responded as best he could. "I'm a pale and bitter man myself, never did see the attraction of Guinness."

"Take it from me, just half a pint of Guinness will have you back on your feet in no time at all and you'll find yourself pelting down this lane faster than you can say Cock Robin, know what I mean, Rudolph?" and he leant over and gave Rudolph an obvious wink with his left eye and a nudge which had the effect of almost drowning the poor old man. But Rudolph is a hardy and tenacious sort of man and has the ability to resurface when you least expect it.

"No, Bartok, I've no idea what you're talking about," he spluttered. "I have no desire to swim like Cock Robin at all."

"Think of the ladies, Rudolph, think of the ladies! You'll take their breath away with such improved performance! They won't be able to take their eyes off you. You'll be working your way up that lane so quick, they'll have to get out of your way, or better still, you'll be able to overtake them and send them a quick wink whilst you're at it. All down to a pint of Guinness!

"Thank you, Bartok, but my days with the ladies are over. And between you and me..." he leant over to Bartok – who had splayed himself out on the poolside – and whispered something in his ear which caused Bartok to pull himself together and a look of concern to wash over his craggy face. I couldn't quite make out what he had said to Bartok but it had quite an effect.

"Well, I think that's me done for today," he announced, whilst adjusting his watch's settings. That looks like a monthly record to me, if I say so myself, so if you'll excuse me, Rudolph, it's time for me to get on with my day and rub the old bear down a bit before I get back to the coalface. Have a good day!"

"Never mind the day! Have a great time! All the time!" Rudolph duly responded and the two had a friendly chuckle as Bartok heaved himself out of the pool and headed off to the changing rooms whilst Rudolph struck out again for at least one more length. I don't know what possessed me, but I got the urge to follow Rudolph back to the changing rooms. I quickly signalled to Beatrice across the pool that I had to make an urgent exit in the direction of the changing rooms and she acknowledged my imminent departure. I had an inexplicable feeling that Bartok would head for my cubicle so needed to get into place before him. I needn't have worried though; he was holding forth in the public showers again to a few disinterested swimmers who were dowsing off the chlorine from their tired bodies.

"Of course, it's important that you properly warm down after a long swim, particularly in a pool like this where the water temperature can fool the body into thinking it's colder than it actually is. As you continue your swim, the body redirects the blood flow to protect its inner organs which makes you feel colder than you actually are: so, when you stop you are at a real risk of overheating, which of course increases the risk of a stroke, embolism or even, the Lord Almighty forbid, a heart attack. I take great care myself to avoid such an outcome by spending a few minutes in the shallow end undertaking some simple stretches and lunges– oh!" He looks up at this point to see that the swimmers have left him to own devices and that the only person he's sharing his hard-earned wisdom with is Anastasia who is mopping the floors down and slowly heading for the exit.

I am now safely tucked away in my cubicle at this point with the door locked, my feet off the floor on the bench and my head resting against the wall, just in case. Just in case of what, I'm not sure, but it seems like an obvious thing to do. It will stabilise me I feel, just in case there's any untoward movement in the adjacent cubicle. So, I sit tight and am soon duly rewarded. The door of cubicle one crashes open and Bartok makes his grand entrance, throwing his changing bag into the basket, and rifling around in it for his clothes. His shoes get thrown on to the floor, and for some reason he hits the door and locks and unlocks it several times over, perhaps to make sure that no one else can get in. Then, surprisingly, silence descends upon cubicle one. This is an unnerving experience when you think that it's Bartok who has taken up residence in the cubicle and I soon wonder whether my ears have deceived me and am tempted to get down off the bench and go back to my duty. But in the nick of time, Bartok inadvertently lets his presence be known but, on this occasion, and unbeknownst to him, it's just to me, rather than the whole pool and it's in the smallest, meekest voice that I have ever heard:

"In the name of the Father, and of the Son, and of the Holy Spirit. Amen. Bless me, Father, for I have sinned."

And that's it. I strain to hear more, but to no avail. He's either thought better of it or been distracted, I can't tell. I have an impulse to answer him but stop myself just in time: Petr is calling my name in somewhat of a state of urgency, so I rush out of cubicle two before

Bartok has had a chance to open the door, and I head towards the likely outcome of being slagged off by Petr.

8. One Less Trainee

The siren wails of Petr, Monica, and Anastasia all greeted me when I reached poolside, along with the sight of our resident mermaid, sat at the water's edge, shivering, her long legs dangling into the choppy waters. The cleaning regime had just started and something was clearly amiss.

You would see the mermaid usually diving for what I assumed would be pearls in the deep water of the pool, minding her business by not getting in the way of the lane hogs, turtles and other sea creatures which would wend their ways back and forth during their swimming session. Not content with being a dolphin, like some of her peers, instead she would repeatedly dive to the bottom of the deep-end and search for what I presume were oysters or coral reef or some other exotic treasure which us poor landlubbers could only imagine. The water certainly wasn't clean enough to discern exactly what it was she was looking for. She would repeat it time and again, staying longer each time, spinning and turning and luxuriating in the clear-ish blue-ish water, and clearly looking exasperated every time she surfaced. Was this because she was vexed at having to surface for air, having found her natural domain at the bottom of the pool? Or was it because she still couldn't find what she looking for? Those elusive oysters? Angel fish perhaps, or even a lost wedding ring? Whatever it was she still hadn't found it at the end of the session and today, Anastasia had to ask her politely to leave the pool once the bell had rung.

Well, politely and Anastasia don't really belong in the same sentence but Anastasia was only doing her job to the best of her considerable vocal ability, and I'm just sorry that the mermaid didn't recognise that she was doing her job, and saving her life from a fate considerably worse than drowning: that of being sucked unceremoniously into the pool's cleaning system which was extremely noisy and clanky at the best of times. It hadn't been repaired in well over a year and every time it started up at the end of a session, it sounded like the entire building was going into a kind of mechanical spasm. The kind which you wouldn't have been surprised to see the pool bed crack open up to reveal the gates of hell firing on all cylinders, cogs and wheels ablaze in furious fiery torment, ready to drag down any poor unfortunate swimmers who had outstayed their welcome in the slow lane to an unimaginable death.

"Anastasia was just doing her job," I said in her defence at her hearing with Petr and Monica. But they were having none of it and sacked her on the spot.

"The customer is always, *always* right!" they countered Anastasia's protest that the mermaid had contravened the regulations. Shame really as she only had 21 days to go before passing her probationary period, but Petr and Monica were hard taskmasters who had lost their collective souls somewhere along their way to senior management. It did at least mean though that there was one less trainee to worry about when it came to the end of the month and the decision as to who would get the job of a lifetime; that of saving the souls at the Day One Leisure Centre.

9. The Holy Trinity

I'm guessing that I should probably take some of the blame for Anastasia's sacking. If I hadn't left the pool to follow Bartok, and asked her to cover for me, then she would never have gotten into that row with the mermaid. I would have dealt with that situation more sympathetically and not made such a big issue of the regulations. She could have dived for pearls a bit longer; Anastasia could have reined in her tongue a bit and no one would be any the wiser. On the other hand, Petr and Monica would have made short shrift of me when they realised that I wasn't exactly playing by the regulation rule book; and, more than likely, it would have been me staring at the gym front doors, P45 in hand, consoled only by you seagulls here in the leisure centre car park.

Quite what you make of it all, God only knows but I suspect you neither know not care. All you're bothered about is where the next chip papers are coming from isn't it? Scavenging for your next meal and certainly no interest at all in career choices or what you do with the rest of your scratty lives on this planet. I don't really know why I'm talking at you at this time in the morning anyway. It's way too early for anyone, least of all an apprentice guarder of lives. I should be back at home, wrapped up in my duvet, checking out my socials rather than muttering to you lot.

But actually, I do know: I need to make a good impression on those in power, those who could determine my future with one tap on their keyboard which could send me back to the hell pit I climbed out of five months ago. You lot think you've got it tough? You should try being me these days. So, I'm here, bright and early, ready to make my mark on the good citizens of the community, assisting them in their every customer need and paying heed to their every concern and confession. The former I'm struggling with, given they're such a cantankerous bunch of demented denizens from the deep, the latter I'm getting the hang of and have a sense of this being my USP as they say in the business awareness classes we attend as part of my qualification. Life guarding is nothing if it's not knowing your USP, calculating your value and knowing what your return on investment is to your employer these days. It's a tough holy trinity to live up to, but live up to it I shall.

10. My USP?

I was a bit of an actor at secondary school and was renowned for attempting to play parts in which I was well out of my depth. Alcoholics, thugs, kings, the list went on and after a while I thought I was being type cast into every difficult role going. Not only cast, but also fully expected to fail in those roles, asking as they did for an imaginative capacity which stretched well beyond my daily experience of being a nice suburban boy in a nice suburban home with every daily comfort that could be imagined.

But one thing I did manage to master through those multiple failures, was to disguise my voice by pretending to be a lot older than I was. Even at the age of thirteen, I managed a credible 90-year-old's timbre; if you shut your eyes and didn't listen too intently. So, I found myself much in demand for the increasing number of school radio plays, produced on account of the reduction in teaching budgets and the increase of teachers' unwillingness to work beyond 3.30pm.

This peculiar skill got me in and out of hot water on several times, but I always knew deep down that there would come a time in my life when it would be my salvation, rather than a path to hell and damnation. The episodes in cubicle two indicated to me that the moment had arrived. My USP was to become my response to other people's SOSs.

11. Taking Confession

"Where do you think you're off to in such a hurry? Got a plane to catch?" Petr reached out his hand and grabbed my shirt collar before I could make it into the changing rooms at the end of the session.

"Sorry Petr, I've got some kind of stomach bug. My guts are killing me."

"You lot. You don't know the meaning of gut rot. You think you've got problems. You should try being my brother for a day, he really knows about gut rot. You're just one complaint after another aren't you? A litany of aches and pains when you're awake, and dead to the world when you're asleep. Which is much too frequent for my liking…" He went on berating me as he continued to stroll over to the changing rooms, his words leaving a trail of something unpleasant on the floor tiles as he walked. "And don't be long, you're on divider duty."

Divider duty? This was a complete drag. It took forever to get the dividers rolled back properly. If you got the angle all wrong, you'd have to unwind them, pull them back along the pool and start all over again. I really didn't need to do this right now.

"Ok. Won't be long." No point arguing with him. I walked quickly past the communal showers and headed for my cubicle. No one in it, but some-one was in cubicle one. I opened the door, sat myself down and rested my head against the partition, holding my breath in anticipation. I didn't have to wait long.

"She was walking down the aisle between the cubicles, light grey towel around her shoulders, dripping wet, blonde hair tied tightly back, eyes looking down to the floor, a vestal virgin walking to the altar. I couldn't believe my eyes." It was Rudolph again, quietly muttering to himself. "Look away, look away, just look away". Here goes I thought, and slowly releasing my breath, as if coming up for air from the bottom of the pool, I found an old voice – belonging to, I think, my first teacher in primary school.

"Enter here to wash away your sins. For here is a hospital and not a court of law. Do not be ashamed to enter; be ashamed when you sin, but not when you repent."

Silence on the other side. I have to say I was quite impressed. I had no idea that that old teacher was still lurking somewhere inside me. The silence was suffocating but I had to take another breath before completely collapsing on the floor. But then there was a whisper.

"Thank you."

And with that, Rudolph opened his cubicle door and left the changing rooms as fast as his bent-up body would allow. I waited until I heard no more and then quickly and quietly headed back to my duties poolside.

"Guts got your garters?" shouted Petr from the other side of the pool. "Get over there now and start pulling. We're running late thanks to the state of your insides."

"Yes, Petr, sorry Petr." I almost skipped across the surface of the pool, I was so elated at my vocal prowess. Where might this lead? Who else could I encounter in cubicle two? How long could I get away with it?

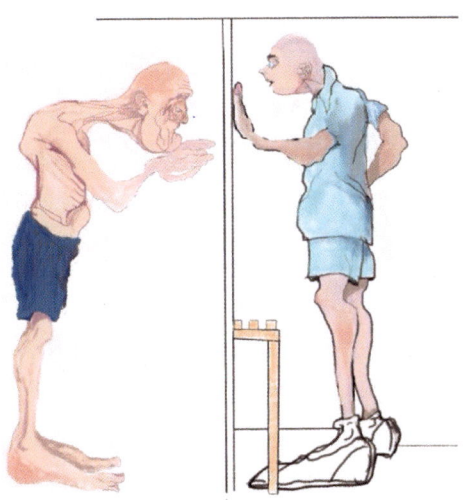

12. The Sermon in the Cubicle

"The human body is truly a terrible thing. We dress it up, perfume it, try to knock it into shape but try as we might, there's no getting away from the fact that it must be one of God's ugliest creations. And you realise this the moment you step into a swimming pool changing room. Gone are the expensive trainers, the sleek leggings, the branded crop top and the Ray Bans: in their stead are the flat feet, the varicose veins and cellulite, the infuriating ever expanding belly and the short sight which has us peering into the middle distance where we think we hear the call of the water and the possibility of shielding and redemption. We totter off to the poolside, our dignity held intact by our budgie smugglers and sleek tinted goggles, but nothing can hide from us the realisation that we are truly ugly beasts, fit for nothing other than to counter our inadequacies by dressing ourselves up daily as if in preparation for Christmas. We consol ourselves with the belief that at least everyone else is like this, that we were all created in God's image and that this a very levelling, reassuring belief until we meet an Adonis or Athena who stroll past us in their flip flops and modest black swim suits which don't exaggerate our pouches or our unseemly spreading bodies which spread in all directions despite our best efforts to maintain an illusion of physical control over our inexorable permanent flaw-lines. And the sheer unpleasant fact is that I hate with my whole heart those figures who emanate perfection from every pore of their oily bodies. Hate them with an unrelenting, unremitting and utterly shameless full force."

At this point I had to let out my withheld breath. It's one thing to have to listen to Bartok extol his physical prowess in the pool, but today, when I was expecting to listen to Rudolph explain his current temptations, all I get is Bartok banging on. It got a bit boring, truth be told, but I summoned my best sympathetic Irish tones and told him that his payment will be in heaven, where all human bodies will be shed, and all our souls will be revealed in all their glory. So, he needn't worry too much about his calorie deficit much longer. Certainly, if he keeps quaffing Guinness in the amount he claims he is used to.

He seemed to accept this with a whispered "Thank you father" and then slid out from his cubicle. The amazing thing is that in the space of just a day, he has got wind of the healing properties of cubicle one, presumably from Rudolph. *Is nothing sacred?* I wonder, as I take care to leave cubicle two, looking around to check for any foreign interference. All clear I mistakenly tell myself, only to bump into Monica who's around the corner, legs astride with that look in her eyes which makes you worry for your immediate safety. I made a sharp exit to the right back towards the sauna to avoid any possible interrogation but she wasn't having any of it.

"Just a moment. I want a word with you, young man."

"Sorry, Monica, scrubbing up duties in the sauna."

"They can wait, come back here this minute…" Her voice trailed off as I fled, working my way around the corridors and before throwing open the sauna door. She couldn't get me in here. We all knew that Monica hated the steam and sweat of the saunas and wouldn't go near them in case they melted her makeup. "Don't think you've got away that easily! I'm coming for you, young Leo, seriously I am!"

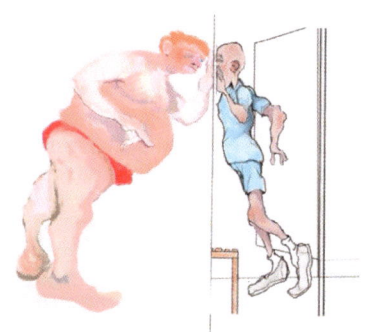

13. Loverley Ladies

Flotsam and Jetsam, as is their wont, had decided to share cubicle one. It's big enough to take them both, a whole family even, so as well as overhearing their conversation, I could hear their various packings and un-packings as they prepared to leave the pool and head back home or to work or wherever it was they were going to next. Jetsam was clearly getting concerned at some unresolved anxiety that had been troubling Flotsam.

"What's up duck?" asked Jetsam in a hushed tone.

"I'm afraid that I wee'd in the pool today. Everyone does it at some time or another in their lives. I didn't mean to; I had prepared myself before I got in the pool. I couldn't help myself. After about 19 minutes I had an urge, that's what it was, a real urge to wee. Non-stop. And so I started but couldn't stop for what felt like years but worst of all, I really enjoyed it.

"Seriously? Enjoyed?"

If I could have seen Jetsam, I would have seen that she had frozen. But I didn't, so I wasn't to know.

"Yes, shocking I know, but I did. And the best thing was, I could swim at the same time."

"You were swimming and peeing–"

"–at the same time, all the way up the fast lane–"

"–all the way up and back?"

"Fifty metres of swimming and weeing."

"That's disgusting!"

It certainly was. Although the idea of the two of them in the fast lane was extreme in itself, I couldn't remember witnessing that particular sight this morning.

"I know, I couldn't help myself. And worst of all... I loved every minute of it. I felt no shame."

Jetsam had clearly had enough at this point. There was the sound of a bag being zipped up vigorously.

"Don't go!"

"I can't listen to this anymore."

"I'm sorry, really I am."

"It's too late now, isn't it? Are you going to tell the lifeguards?"

"I couldn't do that."

"Well, I will then. What you did is disgusting!"

"I'm not that bad." Flotsam was beginning to whine.

"To me you are."

"Oh."

"I don't know what's worse. Peeing in the pool. Peeing in the fast lanes. Or the fact you enjoyed it."

"Don't tell anyone, please."

"Revolting."

"At least I didn't poo!"

"Don't even go there."

Flotsam had clearly hit a previous wound that Jetsam had conveniently forgotten.

"Not like some people I know."

"That was only the once."

"You've forgotten the second time."

"There wasn't!"

"And the third!"

"That was a mistake–"

There was a knock on their door and Beatrice called out to them, concerned. "Are you ladies okay? Anything we can help with?"

"No, it's alright dear," they answered in unison. "Just a bit of difficulty with our costumes. And they giggled.

"Alright, just as long you're both okay. We wouldn't want anything to happen to our 'loverly' ladies now, would we?" Beatrice trilled back in her mock *My Fair Lady* accent.

(Loverly ladies? You should have been where I was sitting, Beatrice, then you'd have heard how "loverly" they were.)

"We'll be fine dear…" continued Jetsam

"Thank you for asking though."

There was a pause as Beatrice's steps could be heard walking away from the cubicles.

"A mistake. Is that the same kind of mistake that happened to your Fred?"

Sharp intake of breath from Flotsam. Sounds of another bag being rummaged through. I couldn't take my head away from the wall.

"Don't you dare mention my Fred. What's done is done–"

"–is done… And you have nothing more to say about him, is that right?"

"Not to you, not to anyone. No."

And with that, the door was thrown open and the two women strode out of the cubicle. I held my breath as if going for a long underwater swim from one end of the pool to the other. When I surfaced, they had gone; no chatter, no steps, nothing.

14. Akupara, all the way

Everyone has their favourite tune first thing in the morning and Oliver the Turtle is no exception. He'll stroll casually to the poolside, large brown towel slung around his neck, humming an infuriating little song in a jaunty style which goes something like: *bom-bom-bombiddy, bombiddy-bom-bom.*

He continues humming whilst disposing of his towel on the floor by the side of the pool – despite having been told many times that he's not allowed to do this and to hang his towel on the hooks like everyone else. He feigns an apologetic smile this morning, as usual, but ignores my instruction (which I have to admit sounds more like a humble request than it does an unequivocal command) and continues to carefully place his flip flops on his towel, to the backing track of *bom-bom-bombiddy, bombiddy-bom-bom*. I swear it's something out of The Dambusters or some other equally military anthem but Beatrice is adamant that it's something from a Disney film.

With flip-flops discarded, he jumps into the middle speed lane in the shallow end. The resulting wave annoys Rudolph, some two lanes away, and causes Bartok to slap the water back at him with his large left hand in a vain attempt to dampen the Turtle's spirits.

He then launches out into the lane, slowly and laboriously, arms in front, legs straight behind him, his body making long slow arches up and out of the water and then back down under the waterline. From the other end of the pool, his resemblance to a turtle is uncanny and his slow progress up the lane does nothing to dispel this impression. This would all be very well in the slow lane, but life in the middle lane is meant for a somewhat faster pace. His wilful ignorance soon causes a backlog of impatient swimmers of varying sizes and shapes, and it's not long before the complaints and curses begin from the swifter and rather irate sea life.

But Oliver pays no attention at all; his rebelliousness is something he clearly cultivates from the moment he enters the pool. The irritating humming, the challenging towel, the rude flipflops, the wrong speed in the wrong lane, all indicate a spirit of someone for whom disobedience is a natural *modus operandi*. I feel a surge of increasing confidence in my ability to challenge him over the error of his ways. I resolve that when he's back in the changing rooms I shall let him know, in no uncertain terms, that his attitude is causing other customers great distress and that he must follow the rules like everyone else. I shall just have to make sure that Petr is nearby too – just in case I need to his reinforcements. He can say what he likes about the customer always, *always* being right, but he also understands the power of numbers. If I can get enough of the irritated sea life lined up in the reception area with their litany of complaints all ready to be released, then maybe, just maybe, Oliver will have no choice but to change his ways and repent. Then none of us will be subjected to his irritating ear-worms – the sea slug that is *bom-bom-bombiddy, bombiddy-bom-bom* – any longer.

15. Early Mornings in Eden

One of the biggest struggles I had during my fledgling career as a life saver in the Day One Leisure Centre, were the early starts to the day. We had to sign in at 5.00am and spend the next 90 minutes prepping the centre for the sluggish customers who wearily pushed their way through the doors, preparing for their next encounter with mortality in the gym, in the pool or the café – that is assuming Gerbil had got up early enough to get his coffee machine functioning.

None of us liked the early starts, particularly those of us who were born on the wrong side of the year 2000 AD. Instead, what we should be doing at 5.30am is getting home from some rave which has lasted the whole weekend somewhere out in deepest Dorset. High off our kites with some newfound friend, who shares the same taste for liquorice in the early hours or has some incomprehensible theory why gravity doesn't exist in the southern hemisphere.

But no, we've found ourselves justifying our career choice (our "next best steps" as they coyly refer to these things in job centres these days) by signing on the dotted line put before us, by what my granddad called, The Man.

Or in my case, Petr.

It's taken me a while to get used to seeing the sun rise over the car park at 5.45am, but it's not a bad sight all things considered. The trees, bushes, the birds; that sort of thing. The colours, the dew, the warm air: all pretty cool really. No sign of any stray party-goers at that time in the morning, although there is the odd stray car abandoned in the car park overnight, presumably because its older-than-me drivers are raving it somewhere in deepest Dorset, enjoying everything that has not been afforded me or my peers. Or pretty much anyone born after the year 2000 AD.

The peace and quiet of this morning, however, is being ever-so-slightly interrupted by the gentle shaking of a Ford Escort parked in the far corner of the car park. I'm intrigued, and once I've checked that neither Petr nor Monica have their beady eyes on me, I move slowly into the car park and towards the car, dodging from tree to tree to make sure I'm not detectable. As I get nearer, the car's movements become a little more urgent and I can see that the windows have misted up too. I'm not sure how the dew has made it into the car so easily but don't bother trying to work it out. The slight shaking becomes a more rigorous rocking and I swear I hear a couple of voices stifling some cries of what can only be described as severe agony. I can make out two voices: one male and one female. Although every now and then I wonder whether I've heard a third, high pitch voice in the mix, also in pain. The rocking suddenly stops, a window opens, emitting steam from within and a hush descends. Then there's a couple of giggles and something tells me I better get back to the reception desk PDQ.

Minutes later, I'm sat at the computer pretending to check-in the customers, when in stroll a couple I've never seen before. Flushed, they look around the reception area in some state of confusion, look at each other and giggle. That same giggle I heard in the car park. The guy presses a finger against his lips whilst looking into his friend's eyes and they both nod, beaming at each other. He steps towards to me.

"Is this the swimming pool? He asked in mock gravitas. Clearly completely off his head but trying to pretend to be as sober as a judge.

"It is," I respond equally gravely, but without the benefit of being off my trolley.

"Marvellous. I'd like two tickets please. How much is that please, my good man?"

"You're not members then?" I ask, stating the blindingly obvious.

"I'm afraid not. Is that a problem?" he looks concerned.

"Not at all. You can either join as an individual now at the knock down price of £150 for the year, or benefit from the couple's discount of £250 which gains you additional access to the Pilates Suite on a Wednesday morning." Petr would have been impressed to see how well I was upselling.

"Oh, no, we're not a couple," he replies, seeming to blush, glancing at his partner who is looking up at the men's swimming costumes "in the usual sense, know what I mean." They grin at each other.

"Yes sir, of course. In which case you can pay a one-off daily membership fee of £20 each for unlimited swimming today." I'm going to extract every last penny I can from them, I thought.

"Well, no, we don't really have time to spend the whole day here. Too many other responsibilities know what I mean." That phrase was beginning to irk me. I didn't know what he meant and wasn't really inclined to find out, given the episode in the car park.

"That's a shame. I understand." I smiled and winked at him, not knowing what I was winking about.

"Look, can't you just let us in for twenty minutes or so? We won't be long." He was getting a bit pushy.

"Well, it's a lane swimming session at the moment and quite busy. Let me check my register." I make a great play at scrolling through various pages on my computer screen, uttering various *ums* and *ahs* and *ers* as I do so. "We can squeeze you in for 30 minutes, but you'll need to wear swimming caps, ear plugs and flip flops. Our hygiene standards are exemplary. Particularly after COVID, you'll understand."

He nods, impatiently. "Ok, that's fine. How much?

"Do you have your own costumes?" He shakes his head. "Well, if you'd like to choose a couple, and leave me your name and addresses, I'll get on with the computer work straight away!" I beam at him. They pay me a grand total of £120 for the session and matching swimwear and minutes later, Mr and Mrs John Smith are walking sprightly towards the changing rooms. I decide I want to see how this plays out and signal Beatrice to come and relieve me from my desk duties.

I think I've done pretty well this morning, having screwed £120 out of them. I wonder if they're going to dare continue the "screwing" act over the next 30 minutes before the bell summons them from the swimming pool and they are ejected them from the premises. This I cannot wait to see.

16. The Deep End

It took me a while to see Mr and Mrs Smith though all the bobbing heads, stretching bodies and flailing limbs which were working their way through the pool that morning. But after my eyes had adjusted to the bright morning sunshine streaming through the windows, they were unmistakable. They had both navigated their way to the far end of the pool – where we were a lifeguard down – and were both resting before returning to the shallow end. Well, "resting" was a bit of a euphemism. If you looked closely, what they were actually doing was anything but resting. They seemed to be in very close contact and were moving rhythmically together, making ripples across the pool in the process. I nudged Beatrice.

"Do you see what I see?"

"I do. They've got a nerve. What do we do?"

"Just watch out for the powers that be. Don't think anyone else has noticed, do you?" She shook her head. We both stood stock still, entranced by the picture developing in front of us. As far as we could tell, everyone else seemed oblivious to what was unfolding; even Flotsam and Jetsam, having finally reached the deep end that morning, made no obvious sign of noticing anything. They had been continuing their arguments about their dinner arrangements right up and under the noses, so to speak, of the Smiths, so perhaps it wasn't surprising they were completely oblivious to the Smith's activities. The ripples became deeper and more frequent as we continued to watch, and soon, Mrs Smith's giggles echoed across the pool from the deep end. Beatrice and I looked at each other again, barely able to stifle our own laughter.

"Well, she's having a grand old time," Beatrice said almost admiringly.

"I guess so. I wouldn't know."

"Wouldn't you…? Surely you would know if…" And she looked intently at me, almost in a state of disbelief. "You mean, you wouldn't know if… your girlfriend was… you know… enjoying your attentions…" She stumbled over the notion of my attentions and I shrugged, shamefacedly, and had to avert my gaze from her. By now, the Smiths were causing a bit of a commotion, and it was difficult to know where to look. The fact is that even at the tender age of 18, I still had not been in a relationship with a member of the opposite sex in which to be able to lavish my attentions upon her. I had got close several times – I told myself privately every now and then – but the move from the first lunge, to the final act, was something that had so far eluded me in my short life.

Not only was I a trainee lifeguard, I felt I was a trainee to life itself, and still to learn about its more intimate mysteries. This was something I was quite equanimous about in private, but obviously, it was something you wouldn't brag about to your mates of either gender in any situation, private or public. And certainly not in a public swimming pool, even if it was called the Day One Leisure Centre.

But if I was short on ideas of how to make this transition from apprentice to fully grown adult, the Smiths were clearly not short of a few examples and working models to learn from. Their cavorting had become more audible now, their machinations more extreme and obvious to the swimmers. I was shocked to see that no one was up in arms about the Smith's behaviour, but on the contrary, they were either in a state of denial (Flotsam and Jetsam) or were actually egging them on (everyone else).

"Go on my son!" you could hear Bartok waving his arm and fist in a manner which could only be referred to as absolutely disgusting. He had climbed out of the pool, and was heading quickly over to the Smiths, trying not to slip into the pool at the same time.

"Is that…? Are they…? My goodness, so they are…" Rudolph had gathered himself in the shallow end and was taking an intense interest in proceedings. I'd never seen him get out of the pool so quickly for anything. Flotsam and Jetsam in the meantime continued their stately pace back to the shallow end, sharing tips on how to poach eggs.

Before long a little crowd had gathered at the far end, looking approvingly at the rutting Smiths.

"'Dogfishing.' That's what it is," Beatrice advised me confidently. Normally people do it in car parks. Never seen it in a swimming pool though, I must say." I looked at her, feeling slightly shocked. She wasn't much older than me, so how come she knew about dogfishing?

"Don't you think we should do something about it?" I felt my career ebbing away, ripple by ripple. "What if Petr and Monica turn up?" I needn't have worried. The dynamic duo had clearly got wind of what was going on and weren't going to accept the Smith's behaviour in their pool. Petr came running to the poolside, having hit the emergency alarm button firmly on the way.

"Right! Everyone out! You! And you! Get out of this pool immediately! Get yourselves dry and clear out of my pool…NOW! Everyone else… today's session is over, get out of the pool and <u>get</u>

yourselves home. This is going to involve one hell of a cleaning bill."
And looking down at the state of the Smiths, you felt Petr had a point.
Their costumes were distressed beyond the point of returning to the
manufacturers and there were strange slimy deposits in the water
which I didn't dare ask anyone what they were, although I had a pretty
good idea, having spent far too long in my bath at home when I was
aged about thirteen.

I rapidly stopped thinking about those earlier years and helped the
customers who (if you remember), were always, *always* right, out of
the pool and back into the changing rooms. I caught sight of the
Smiths locking themselves into cubicle one and just couldn't help
myself. I made my apologies and headed straight for cubicle two,
locked the door behind me and, head on the partition, expectantly
waited for the hubbub to subside.

17. Soz

"Monica says she's raised a PO for the parts. I've raised it with our technical manager Justin who's said he's raised it with the people he needs to raise it with."

"It's like raising the dead."

"I'm sorry about this, sir. Please accept our apologies."

"Soz. Is that all you've got?"

"I'm afraid so, sir."

It was proving to be a difficult couple of days. After the Smiths had been ejected from the premises and the pool itself cleansed of the debris resulting from their Dionysian frolics, the various ageing mechanical processes which ran the entire Day One Leisure Centre had finally succumbed to the inevitable. Several key operational functions began to shut down with barely a moment's notice. First it was the sauna. Then the day after, it was the men's showers. And the day after that... who knows? I lost track of the POs, memos, and the urgent to and fros between the poolside staff and the centre's administrators. The Finance Department seemed to be on a permanent holiday; they weren't answering their phones or responding to emails – despite Petr, his boss, and the boss's boss being cc'd into the email trail.

At the reception desk, I was left having to face increasingly irate customers who had to leave the pool, damp, cold and tousled due to the knock-on effects of the leisure centre's creaking and incontinent infrastructure. And of course, where are your managers when the shit is hitting the fan? Nowhere to be seen of course. For all his certainty about the fool-proof-ness of customers, Petr mysteriously absented himself when they were – quite understandably – asserting their rights and vocalising their opinions about the state of the pool, their contractual rights and our legal obligations.

"It says in my contract that any repairs will be carried out within 24 hours and that I will be compensated for every day after that if repairs are not carried out to a reasonable standard," explained Turtle, for what was definitely not the first time. Nor the last, I suspected. He seemed oddly pleased. Perhaps it was that, finally, he had something legitimate to complain about. Or maybe it was the thought of potential financial reparations.

"Yes, sir, please be assured that we are doing the best we can in the circumstances."

"So how do I apply for my compensation?"

"If you let me your name and email address, then I shall make sure the relevant paperwork is sent over to you." This seemed to have the magical effect of quietening him down.

"OK. It's…"

"One minute, I just need to log in." I made a few professional looking taps of my keyboard and stared at the screen intently. That little magic spinning wheel of death materialised in front of me and my heart sank.

Today? Really?

It seemed that it was now the turn of the IT system to go AWOL. "I'm sorry sir, I seem to have a problem logging in. I'll raise it with my senior straight away and no doubt he will raise a PO to deal with the issue. I'll also raise it with our technical manager Justin who will raise it with the people he needs to raise it with."

Exasperated, Turtle turned and would have fled straight out of the front doors, had he had the wherewithal to flee. Instead, he trundled back into the café, plonked himself down at a table, dropping his sports bag all over the floor and spilling its contents into the bargain.

"Coffee!" he bellowed to no one in particular. Gerbil looked up from his serving hatch, shrugged his shoulders and pulled down the shutter.

Today looked like going from bad to worse.

18. Granny Smith and the Lost Apples

"Granny Smith, is that you?" Seconds later, the hatch is thrown open and Gerbil sticks his angry head out. "Was that you Granny Smith? That everyone's talking about?"

An old woman sat quietly in the corner of the café, trying to disappear into the furniture, shrugs and looks away. She adjusts her sunglasses, picks up her gym bag, puts on her coat and steps toward the exit. Gerbil shouts after her in his increasingly agitated Italo-English accent.

"Such a bad example you are setting the young people with your behaviour. You at your age, you should be knowing better. I'm not serving you again in this café ever again!"

I'm surprised that Gerbil seems to know the miscreant, because as far as I could tell, Mrs Smith and her partner had been complete strangers to the pool community. None of us had seen them before. Yet here was Gerbil with apparent prior knowledge, and what's more, knowledge of the gossip in our community about the two of them. She stops and turns to face him about to respond but checks herself, thinks better of it, and continues towards the front revolving doors. But once inside the slowly spinning airlock, she undergoes another change of mind and swings right back around into the reception area with a point to make.

"Let me tell you Mister Giuseppe, that if anyone in this gym has a clear conscience as far as their behaviour is concerned, they can form a queue to throw the first apple core at me. But if not – and that includes you Mister Giuseppe – then I suggest they and you keep your collective mouths shut and your pointing fingers down by your sides. Otherwise..."

And without further explanation as to what the consequences of their open mouths and up-pointed fingers would be, she swept back into the revolving door, gave it a sharp push and strode back out into the daylight where her partner in swimming pool crime was waiting for her. They embraced, turned their backs on the pool and helped each other back to the car park, tentatively prodding the uneven ground with their walking sticks.

"OAPs?" muttered Gerbil. "More like ROCs. Randy old codgers." And he slammed the hatch down again to stew in his own self-righteousness.

19. The Nephilim

I'd never seen Petr and Monica looking quite so rattled. Their usual sense of authoritative arrogance had evaporated and they were running around like a pair of headless chickens. What was worse, they were being so pleasant to everyone.

"Have you got everything you need to do your job?" Monica asked me in a fever of concern I'd never imagined in her before.

"Tell me," asked Petr of Beatrice, "what barriers are you facing to completing your tasks? What support do you need?"

"And how is your work/life balance?" Monica enquired of Gerbil, through gritted teeth it seemed to me but it gave him the opportunity to wax lyrical about supply chains, food hygiene, customer quality, and how he had never wanted to run a café in the first place, but was forced into it by his demanding wife and could Monica do anything about that?

Beatrice and I watched in growing astonishment as the caring, sharing sides of the dynamic duo became more prevalent in the days following the Smiths and the failing machinery. It was not until Rudolph happened to mutter gnomically in passing, "The inspectorate", that we began to understand.

Of course, it became obvious. Those mysterious figures from HQ would be descending on us from on high to come and sort things out once and for all. Presumably all the complaints had somehow gotten through and action now had to be taken. We both clocked what this meant and enjoyed the attentions of Petr and Monica, positively providing lists of how they could improve our lot at the Day One Leisure Centre.

"And how is your mental health?" Petr asked me almost innocently. This was a question too far and I felt I had no option other than to tell him straight. But before I could open my mouth, there was a flurry of activity at the front revolving door, and one by one four men in black suits spun their way into the leisure centre, laptops in hand, dark glasses in unison.

"Take us to your leader," whispered Gerbil to me but quickly shut up when one of them turned to face him.

"Two cappuccinos. One latte. One cortada. All decaf. Now."

"Don't worry about the scanner guys, just push through." Just when you thought it couldn't get any worse, it did.

Of course it did.

Customers were struggling to get in and out of the centre due to some inexplicable problem with the gates. They were normally operated by scanning your mobile over a sensor which would work out who you were, where you'd been, and how many activity points you'd clocked up in the course of your visit. Today though, the scanners refused to comply, locking everyone who was in, in, and everyone who was out, out. Petr showed a moment of temporary panic by switching them off and advising everyone to just push through.

Cue hiatus. Customers who were members, customers who weren't, to and fro, back and forth, going in every conceivable direction now that the controlling technology had finally given up the ghost.

It was a free for all and there was nothing he or Monica could do about it.

20. The Fog, the Sauna and the Holy Spirit

The sauna. A source of fear, loathing, and intense pleasure for many of the customers, often all at the same time. I couldn't quite figure it out, how such a feature of our leisure centre could conjure such opposite emotions – often in the space of a couple of minutes. Yet attract and repel people it did, in equal measure. I therefore distrusted it immensely and used to try and structure my sessions in such a way that I didn't have to go near it. But this pattern was soon noticed by Petr and Monica, and whether out of curiosity or spite, they began to deliberately timetable me in a way that made sure I prepared, monitored, and cleaned the beast in the corner, all in the same session. If they took great delight in tormenting me this way, I was determined not to show them what anguish they were inflicting upon me.

With the arrival of the inspectors, I thought this would be the ideal time to right the wrongs of my recent scheduling history, set the record straight and get me away from sauna duties for the rest of my career.

"Sauna?" The tallest inspector of the cabal looked down his nose at me disdainfully. "You've been allocated sauna monitoring duties you say? Do you have the relevant health and safety certificate?"

I had to admit I did, but that I was more concerned with my own health and safety because I had suffered from bronchitis as a child and my mum had always warned me to stay away from steam of any description.

"Fog, saunas, autumnal mists…" I explained to him. "Anything that could set me off." And I started a feeble hacking cough to emphasise the point.

"I see. Leave it with me." He turned to his colleagues to confer. They formed a huddle, muttering incomprehensibly and he eventually resurfaced.

"We need to speak," he said pointedly to Petr. "Now." And off Petr and Monica trotted to his office, Monica casting a vengeful eye in my direction.

"Don't forget you've only got ten days left on your probation," she hissed. And with that, they were whisked off to the back offices, gone, never to be seen again.

21. Missing Management

It took Gerbil, Beatrice and me, a full morning to realise what had happened. After Petr and Monica had been taken away to the offices, presumably we thought for a debriefing, we got on with our jobs the best we could. This was made increasingly difficult by the customers who were asserting their rights to be "right" ever more stridently as the list of complaints grew.

"The taps in the shower rooms are permanently on," moaned Flotsam to Jetsam. "Think of all that water going to waste. What are they going to do about it?"

"At least everything's getting a good clean," responded her twin. "It's amazing how some things need washing and washing and washing..." Her voice faded as Jetsam stared at her, refusing to continue the conversation.

"Have you found my lost towel? enquired Rudolph of Beatrice. "I had it not five minutes ago and it seems to have disappeared off the face of the earth." She sympathised and suggested she look through his bags which he firmly rejected. "No need for that, I can manage quite nicely thank you." She shrugged and turned her back on him, only to be confronted by a bellicose Bartok.

"I'm red hot in here. Can't you turn the heating down? You'll give us all heart attacks." Bartok's high horse was beginning to stamp its hooves again. "You wait until I see my GP. My blood pressure is going through the roof! I only come here to get fit and healthy, at least, that's what he advised me to do. But look at me, I'm sweating like a stuck pig!"

He had a point; he did look much the worse for wear and I began to worry that we might have a medical incident on our hands before too long.

"OK, look just sit down and have a nice glass of iced water." I beckoned for Gerbil to supply him pronto and he duly obliged. "That's it, you'll feel better in a minute."

"I should bloody hope so. Don't want to be dying in your nice clean foyer now, do I?"

"Quite." I looked around for some assistance, remembering that my health and safety certificate wasn't quite up to date and that I hadn't fully mastered CPR just yet.

But the management duo was nowhere to be seen.

"What a great way to start the day," he leant over to Rudolph.

"Never mind the day! Have a great time! All the time!" Rudolph duly responded but with a bit less conviction than usual.

"Quite so." And at that point, Bartok went bright red in the face and fell off his chair, clutching his chest.

I started to panic.

"Is there a doctor somewhere? Can someone phone for an ambulance? Er… what do we do…?"

"You're the lifeguard, you save him," Gerbil muttered scornfully from behind me.

"Thanks, Gerbil. Very helpful." I got down on my knees and did what I thought best.

Started to pray.

22. The Power of Prayers and Defibrillators

I'd not prayed since I was at school all those years ago when praying came naturally or at least, by routine. I would pray not to get picked on by our class teacher, not to have to answer any questions, not to have a view on anything, and not to be noticed for my free school dinner which was always waiting for me in the dining room, set slightly apart from most of my mates' meals.

But as it turned out, praying came back surprisingly easily.

"Dear God. Don't take Bartok just yet. I have my probation to complete. I need a job. I need a career. This is my best chance. This is the only chance I'm going to get ever again. If you take him, it'll be my fault and I'll be slung out of here as soon as you can say 'P45'. I know he's a bit overweight, but he has promised to get healthy and he's doing a great job as far as I can tell. So don't take Bartok. You don't need him just yet. He's needed down here. I need him down here. Please."

And joy of joys, Bartok's face twitched, one eye opened and he looked at me.

"I know you." he whispered. "You're the one in the cubicle." And with that, his massive body gave another violent shudder.

"Stand back, stand back!" the cavalry had arrived in the shape of Beatrice. She had not only found the defibrillator but was clued up enough to be able to operate it, without having to refer to the instructions at the same time. To say I was impressed wasn't the half of it; I think I fell in love for the first time ever at that point. Several shocks later and amidst many gasps and *oohs* and *aahs* from the assembled shoal of customers, Bartok was sitting up again, a healthier shade of pink, and being given a great deal of care and attention by his saviour, Beatrice.

I watched him to see if he would catch my eye, hoping that he had forgotten what it was he had whispered to me. But he was too busy basking in the crowd's attention to concern himself with me, so I took the opportunity to slip out of the centre's revolving doors and head over to the seagulls in the car park.

They'd know what to do next.

23. Before the Flood

To my dismay, the car park was bereft of seagulls. They'd flown away, every single one of them, leaving not a trace of their presence. Well, apart from the stray chip papers that is, which blew aimlessly across the ground, wrapping themselves around lampposts, parked bicycles or the abandoned outdoor gym equipment. I wandered over to the rusting shoulder press and tried my luck; but I soon gave this up as a bad idea. I didn't like the *indoor* gym equipment at the best of times, and this sullen outdoor kit didn't fill me with any newfound motivation for pressing, pushing or curling – or any activity which required me to exert myself beyond my usual comfort level. "No pain, no gain!" our instructors would exhort us to remember during our training and I always wondered whether that trade off was all it was cracked up to be.

It began to rain.

I returned to the centre, and nodded farewell to the customers who had purged themselves for the day and, in pairs, were making their ways back home, to work, or to their future destinies no matter what they were. I knew I had to face up to mine and made my way to the scene where I last saw Bartok, lying adoringly in the arms of Beatrice, his saviour and now lifelong poolside buddy.

For the first time I felt a twinge of what I assumed was jealousy; Beatrice would win the acclaim of the customers, the attentions of Bartok and probably the one job we were both fighting for. I would be left with nothing apart from a glowing reference and the opportunity to start all over again at a job centre of my choice. From the lofty heights of being a trainee lifeguard and redeemer of souls, I would become a mere customer again, all because I had no idea how to operate a defibrillator and save lives in the most obvious of ways: keeping their hearts ticking over.

I sat down at one of the café tables and looked around to see what was left for me, only to see some water spreading slowly across the floor from the changing rooms. Slowly it crept, inexorably, tolerating no borders, ignoring all barriers, towards the reception, the gym, the activities hall and horror of horrors, the dry changing rooms.

As I looked around for assistance, it dawned on me that there probably wouldn't be enough mops to stop this flood. But there was not a soul to be seen anyway, and I realised that this was to be my moment; my vocational call to potentially save the swimming pool itself, from itself. So, despite a huge urge to either run away or curl up and go to sleep there and then, I ran towards the source of the rising tide, into the changing rooms to find the source of this impending flood: cubicle two.

24. That Sinking Feeling

I'd seen the film, *Titanic*, several times over the years of my early childhood, usually at Christmas or those public holidays when there was nothing else to do but to witness disasters on a monumental scale behind the safety of the small TV set we had in our family flat. Like many people, I felt the best bit was when the boat was hit by the iceberg and started its long stately process of sinking, with all the attendant chaos raining down on the microcosm of humanity that was thrashing around in the boat.

"Serves you bloody well right!" we all cheered as the toffs got their comeuppance. "Didn't see that coming, did you?" We'd remark unnecessarily as the captain flailed around the deck issuing ineffective orders to anyone who had bothered to stay with him. "Good on ya!" we cheered the Serbian musicians who were determined to play their national folk song to the bitingly bitter end. "Oh, just get on with it!" we'd shout at Rose and Jack as they managed to find the most difficult route out of the boat, forgetting all their possessions and keepsakes. Did no one tell them to leave their laptops and mobile phones behind (or whatever the 1912 equivalent was: lockets and typewriters?), rather than search for them at the most inconvenient of moments?

25. Après moi, le déluge

It wasn't a dramatically forceful flow, just a steady stream from a couple of pipes which had inexplicably ruptured through the back wall and were now spewing their contents in a slow but relentless fashion. I knew that plugging the holes with cotton wool wasn't an option this time. Drilling a peephole and stuffing it with a temporary filling was one thing: but this was another order of magnitude and, this time, I honestly couldn't claim any responsibility for it.

At first, I rapidly shut the cubicle door in a vain attempt to stem the flow but in the best Titanic tradition, this achieved nothing. The water continued to seep under the door and there were signs of it leaking through the gap between the door and the adjacent wall. And then, curiously, the water started to reveal lost treasure; pieces of coral, oysters, a wedding ring. All were unceremoniously deposited on the floor at my feet. The mermaid had been right all along. I could at least tell her, if I got out of here alive, that her endeavours weren't in vain. I pocketed the wedding ring just in case I saw her again.

There must be a stop cock around here somewhere, I reckoned in a flash of insight, and rushed through the changing rooms to try and find it. Frogs, angel fish, newts all swam by. Where they had come from God only knew: I didn't realise we had such a vibrant ecosystem in the basement of our modest swimming pool. I ran into the gent's changing rooms and opened a toilet door in search of the stop cock and was met by what could only be described as a tsunami of shit.

I gagged, and tried to shut the door behind me, but it was too late, the tsunami had found its opening and the shit was released. It was all I could to wade out of the rising water levels and rush towards the women's changing rooms. Dare I go in there at such a time? It was too late to worry about the proper protocols, so I plucked up the chutzpah and ran in there too – chased by the shit from the men's toilets.

No sign of a stop cock there either.

The sauna.

Perhaps that would be the safest place to be. It had higher ground after all. So now wading through the waters and surrounded by leisure centre debris of life jackets, inflatables and arm bands, I headed to the saunas with the water an ever-increasing resistance to my mission. For some reason, the sauna had yet to be inundated. Perhaps it was the plinth it was installed on which gave it temporary protection, perhaps its heat was fending off the flood, who knows? I was just happy to get in and slam the door behind me.

"About time too!" Turtle announced, sat there with nothing on except his pink flipflops. "Where have you been? Do you know how long I've been waiting for to someone to fix the bloody thermostat? Call yourself a public swimming pool? And look at you – you're a disgrace!" I had to admit he was right but didn't have time to explain.

"There's a flood… the pool is leaking…" I tried explaining.

"Flooding my arse. I'll show you a flood." And with that, he strode out of the sauna, stark bollock naked, and towards the lockers, pulling open Locker 123 he retrieved a wrench and waved it aloft, triumphant. "That'll fix it." He'd found the stopcock. I could breathe again.

"How did you know where the stop cock was?" I asked him later when we'd been able to clean up and Gerbil had reopened the café."

"Simple." he said, but he didn't give anything away. There was a tapping at the café window. One of the seagulls had returned and was looking for food again. If they only knew I thought. All those fish they'd missed. Right under their noses, if they'd just been patient.

26. Back to Sleep

Needless to say, I didn't complete my probation period. The leisure centre closed for six months on account of the flood, and consequently, the ever-distant management had no need for two trainee lifeguards or soul savers and dismissed both of us straight away – not even letting us work our notice period. Which was a bummer, seeing as we were just a few days away from Christmas and I'd been hoping to enjoy the festivities of the season. The works' parties, the hangovers, the family arguments and all those other great things about Christmas, when you're in work: the bank holidays, the mindless TV and the sense of existential anguish between Christmas and New Year. But none of this was to be mine, at least, not this year. I packed my final bag, bade Beatrice farewell and suggested we might meet up at some point in the future. She smiled and nodded which meant that I'd never see her again.

Back to sleep, I thought.

27. A Full Leg of Lamb

In the end, we did manage to organise one seasonal festivity between us all, and I was grateful to be able to keep in touch with some of the community I had been part of during those early morning swimming sessions. Viv and Ethel (as I found Flotsam and Jetsam were named) organised a little get together one lunchtime and brought some lamb and mint sauce sandwiches along. She confided in me that that her twin, Ethel, was no longer able to visit the pool on account of her missing husband, Fred. There were rumours that he had been found battered to death and stored in the freezer of the family home with a motorcycle chain around his neck. Some say a full leg of lamb was involved, but the rumour mill that is social media is a terrible thing, and these days you can't be quite sure who or what to believe.

The sandwiches were pretty good though.

Gerbil rustled up some wholewheat mince pies which tasted disgusting but were still much appreciated. The mermaid (whose name I never learned) sat uncomfortably, her covered legs hidden away underneath a table, but appreciative of the fish morsels that Rudolph occasionally threw to her. Beatrice and Bartok sat close by each other, him looking at her adoringly and her patting his arm. It could have been a Christmas card picture; it was such a sickening sight to see. Turtle continued to find fault, but no one minded too much given he had probably saved everyone's lives as a result of his rebelliousness and sheer bad manners.

Me? I was just pleased to be accepted into this odd little collection of humanity in time for Christmas, grateful that no questions could be asked and no answers provided. True, there would be no more confessions: Rudolph's and Bartok's secrets were safe with me, and my carpentry and confessional skills safe with them.

For the time being at least.

End

AND IN THE END...

Panel 1. The Walrus's Tale

I am The Walrus. Goo goo g' joob.

I hear you tenors mutter but no amount of back chat is going to detract me from the fact that I am indisputably The Walrus. Not a walrus, not any old walrus but The Walrus. So listen up, pay attention and learn fast. We've got three hours to turn you miserable lot into a golden angelic host of Serabim and Seraphim so there's no time to waste.

I am the egg man, you are the egg men. Yes, you at the back, keep up. No, it's not red men, blue men or any other sort of men other than of the egg variety.

Altogether now. I am he as you are he as you are me and we are all together. Ladies: keep it together please, this is no time to query the theological nature of the carol. Just accept it for what it is. Pardon? I have no idea what it is, I am just The Walrus, I know nothing other than how to whip together a scratch choir in the time it takes to shake a llama's tail.

Now, a tempo please. Sitting on a cornflake, waiting for the van to come. That's right you basses... Mind the accidentals... Steady now... Enunciate Mr. McCartney, you're not in a bloody grunge band now lad... Cor-por-ation tee-shirt, stu-pid bloo-dy Tues-day. Man, you been a naughty boy, you let your face grow long. Do I really have to spell it out for you?

Yellow matter custard, dripping from a dead dog's eye. What's the matter Mrs Lennon? Distasteful? When have Christmas carols ever been anything but distasteful? They're all about global warming, homeless men and illegitimate births so a dash of dead dog's eye has nothing on Good King Wenceslas.

Ok. Mrs Piano, hang back and get yourself a mince pie or something. Let's just tap this out slowly on our knees shall we, just to feel it before we hurtle our way through it. Wait for it, wait for it... 2, 3, 4, and Crabalocker fishwife, pornographic priestess, excellent let's go for it boy you been a naughty girl you let your knickers down. Superb, superb.

Ok, ok, ok let's hold it there. Mrs Harrison, what seems to be the problem with you and Mrs Starkey? No Mrs Harrison, I am the egg man, they are the egg men. That's right, egg men. I don't know, just use your imagination.

Semolina pilchard, climbing up the Eiffel Tower. They're breath marks Mr Geldorf, they're telling you where to breath.

Elementary penguin singing Hari Krishna. Hold it, hold it. And your problem Mr Bono is what? No problem? Are you sure? Are you quite sure? Are you really, really sure that you'd rather not be standing up here being me? Being the Walrus and master of all you survey? Quite sure? Ok, well shut it from now on. And 2, 3, 4…

Man, you should have seen them kicking Edgar Allan Poe. I am the egg man, they are the egg men.
I am the walrus, goo goo g'joob g'goo goo g'joob.
And coda, once more with feeling.
Goo goo g'joob g'goo goo g'joob g'goo.
Yes, even you Mr Bono.
Goo goo g'joob g'goo goo g'joob g'goo.
Oompah oompah stick it up your jumper
Goo goo g'joob g'goo goo g'joob g'goo
Goo goo g'joob g'goo goo g'joob g'goo.

Job done ladies and gents. This is your half hour call. Mr Bono – I need to see you in my vestry please. Now.

Panel 2. The Goldfish's Tale

I am a goldfish and we get a very bad press. There are those who accuse us having very short memories; there are those who accuse us of... Well, I forget what it is they accuse us of, but it's not especially complimentary.

But what those fish forget in their accusations about our suspect collective memory is that we have compensations which can only be described in the written word because were we to rely on our oral storytelling skills we would fail miserably because... Well, we would just because. I forget why.

These compensations I refer to: they sometimes beggar the imagination. They take all shapes and sizes; they surprise, shock and entertain in equal measure.

Today for example I was swimming around and around looking for something that was hugely important at the time, when quite by chance, out of the blue and completely unexpectedly, I saw myself staring at myself, mouth slightly agape.

This was a revelatory moment as I don't remember ever having had that experience before. Had I ever seen myself before? What was it that had brought about this moment of enlightenment? What did it all mean?

"No"; "no idea", and "not a clue" were the only answers I could summon up and it seemed I would be destined to wait a long, long time before I would be able to figure it all out.

I do recollect though, that the vision of loveliness that faced me quite took me aback. I hadn't realised quite how lovely a colour orange could be. I hadn't appreciated how gossamer thin my magnificent tail was. I was astounded to see me floating effortlessly: bobbing slightly yes, but still maintaining a steady float. How did I do that? I mused.

For a few moments I was one happy goldfish, although it wasn't too long before that feeling passed and I settled back into a vague sense of dissatisfaction with my lot in life. Quite why, I don't know. I don't even know if I knew at some point but then forgot. Perhaps that was the root of my disappointment with myself.

I firmly resolved to address this seeping unease as soon as I could and certainly before I next encountered myself and my awesome loveliness.

And then… Now, where was I?

Panel 3. The Mole's Tale

I am a mole and I live in a hole with the voles of despondency. Cheer up I say, it may never happen but the voles continue to fret in their usual way, whiskers a-quivering, noses a-twitching, feet a-tingling. "You just don't understand" they squeak, "we're doomed, we're all doomed and you mole are first in line when the revolution unfolds."

First in line for what I ask them, but they give me no answer other than to continue their frantic racing through the burrows along the riverbank and out into the estuary. They're preparing for Armageddon and nothing and no-one, not even a mole in a hole is going to stop them.

This morning one of them stopped her twitching and her quivering, sat up straight and looked me straight in my blind eyes and asked in a voice several octaves higher than was comfortable "And where do you think you're going? Heaven or hell? Come the day of reckoning, what side will your bread be buttered Mr Mole?"

I couldn't answer her rhetorical question but continued to dig away at the tunnel I was creating in front of me. She took my silence as a sign of assent for further interrogation. "And do you think digging the same old way is going to get you anywhere at all, mole? Do you really think you are on a path to redemption? Do you not see that your path is the path of the damned? No, I see you see nothing at all and that is the way it should be. God moves in mysterious ways and you, mole, are the most mysterious creature of them all."

Coming from a vole who lives in a hole of despondency struck me as being a bit rich, but I was saying nothing. Hear no evil, speak no evil, dig no evil is my motto and as a mole's mantra goes this is better than most.

"What are you waiting for mole?" She continued. "You cannot wait much longer before the rains come, the river is flooded and we will all be washed away in a flood of hellfire water a-fizzing and a-popping. "I'll take my chance" I said to her and continued to paw away at the tunnel that was forming ahead of me. That's the good thing about being a mole. You make your tunnels; you don't rely on the voles of despondency to do it for you.

The Mole's Tale

Panel 4. Christmas Shopping

O Sprawling Cityscape of Bethlehem

Hither, thither, ant trails along the boulevards
Wrestle wrassle, antennae quivering,
Thieving their way through fluid molten lines of bustle
Along the hedgerows of humankind
Who push and pull, scream and shout, yell and twist
Legs between waists and necks, ankles and fists
Yelling mine! That's mine!
All mine!

Mining for gold on a wet autumn-winter afternoon,
A man has forgotten, temporarily,
Who he is and where he comes from.
He slumps into drab leaf slush, mashed down for a good
 night's rest.
A party hat betrays a recent past:
Burger King-man waits for a guardian angel to collect and set
him on his way.
Help the homeless he mutters but don't help me.
I do have some vestige of manhood about me. Somewhere.

He mutters, searching in vain.

We (are) Three Kings of Leyton Orient, (aren't we)?

Not one, but a cluster of stars:
Orion's Belt, they say, although no-one knows
Whether Orion had trousers to provide solace for his belt.
Or not.
No beasts of burden at the stable either,
No waiting donkey ready to bear lodestones of ivory,
malachite or emerald,
No shepherds tending goats,
Or wise women haunting the ghostly plains of Arimathea.

Yet all surface, sweating profusely at the empty stable.
"So what now?" mutters one,
Tetchy boar-pig knocks into legs; unguarded, unwanted,
 unbidden:
"Any room at the Inn?"
Behind those gilded windows, the tinsel, the glitter of all our
 yesterdays
Contravenes the staple diet of poverty:
There is apparent rest.
"Come on in, there are plenty of rooms!"

They came, they saw, they wondered.

Unto the U.S. a Boy is Born

A stealth bomber scurries out from the bedsheets,
In amongst the shops, planning revenge for an age-old hurt
Which she will put right,
Making all swell in the world.
Cast sin out where none existed,
Caste in iron, she bides her time until the shops shut,
The shutters are shopped and the liquor store closes
(which it never does).

She faces the twenty-four-hour majesty of the out of town
Streetlight lined megalopolis that is the retail site.
The square bakery, the odd bins,
The garden centre for spiritual aspiration.
The pleadings for national unity,
The thin-as-ice wafer-tokens, dispensed to impoverished
school children
From far-off, nearby streets,
An agora for the anxious.

And yet: a secret whispered through our ages resists
conclusion.

A Many Happy No-Returns Policy

And yet we step, trembling, closer to that seventh age,
With Burger King-Man, trouser-less Orion and stealthy
bombette all,
Blind but with partial misty-vision,
Deaf but with extra sensory perception which supersedes
Our default ignorance.
Frustrated at what is,
Sorrowful at what has been,
Anxious about what might be.

These are not the thoughts to enter Christmastide with.
But as the service unfurls,
The yearning, sonorous Christmas cadences probe tenderly
The membrane of those hurts expressed, yet un-expressed.
The spirit of possibility reveals our harbour,
Making that what has been, more settled.
Making that what is, more comforting.
And that what will be, less fearful.

Amen.

Panel 5. The Llama's Tale

I am a llama, currently sat on a hillside, soaking up the warmth from what's left of the setting winter sun. It's not unpleasurable. In the neighbouring field a few ragged old sheep graze their days away, oblivious to their impending fate. It must be one of the benefits of being a sheep: you're permanently oblivious to what's around the next corner.

Being a llama, however, requires you to be in a permanent state of alertness. It's why our necks are so long: we're always looking for the next opportunity, the next big deal, the next time the farmer wanders into the neighbouring field to herd together his oblivious sheep so that they can be carted off to the nearest abattoir. If sheep had longer necks and spent more time looking up into space rather than staring down at their feet, they might be a little less oblivious, a bit more alert and more likely to survive the next visit by the machete wielding farmer.

Today's a case in point. I'm sat here, soaking up the warmth, stretching my neck, and lo and behold, what do we have drop down from the heavens? Only a host of bloody golden guardian angels blowing their trumpets, strumming their zithers and creating a God Almighty din. The sheep – naturally knowing nothing of what is happening – continue to graze amongst the heavenly host, three of whom are gathered around a satnav. They're clearly lost; they scratch their heads, twizzle their beards and gesticulate at each other in a bit of a temper. One of them snaps his zither in two over the back of one of his compadres. There's a bit of a guardian angel fracas.

The sheep remain oblivious to all the commotion apart from a couple of the brighter ones who look up and run off, startled at the sight of quarrelling guardian angels wielding acoustic instruments at each other.

Me, I'm sat here in the warmth of the setting winter sun, waiting for the noise to die down. Once they come to their collective angelic senses, I'll tell them what they want to know.

The Llama's Tale

Panel 6. The Ant's Trail

I am an ant and I move in mysterious ways. Not only am I an ant, but you are an ant too, we are ants and they are ants, in case you were wondering. In fact, I am not so much an ant but Ant: you too are not so much an ant but Ant; we and they too are Ant.

I/we weave my/our trails up sunny hillside and down dusky dale, up and under fishy pet shop and over and through derelict railway station, trailing my/our scent in all corners, leaving no hoof unsullied by our probing antennae, no goldfish bowl un-rimmed by our Ant-ness, no detritus left uninspected by our unending inquisitiveness.

I/we taste all around me/us and glue together all the disparate voices and noises with our invisible slime trails, visible only to those who have Ant-Spectacles, obtainable from all top-quality high-street opticians.

We're weaving a tapestry of Ant glue across the earth, ready for the moment to catch you when you fall and then spring you back up on your feet, waiting for your next steps in Ant World.

The Ant's Trail

Panel 7. The Pigeon's Tale

I am a pigeon, a regular boy pigeon who jauntily hops along railway platforms looking for the next bird to pull... Ooo there she is, hang on lady, just let me get a bit closer... dammit, she's flown the coop.

Never mind, here I am, a regular boy pigeon who's got a bit on the side, a bit back at base, a bit on the front and several bits of fluff scattered around this derelict railway station just waiting for me to fluff their tails, coo sweet nothings at them all night long and then hop off before the going goes from good to soft and from soft to swamp-like.

Cos as a fully paid up boy pigeon I am not partial to birdy ladies who coo and sweat and then angrily swish their tail feathers when little ol' me tells 'em that the time has come for me to fulfil my potential and explore new lands and lady birdies, they don't like it a bit... Ooo there's another one now... 'Ello darlin', how can I be 'elpin' you... Just stand still for a minute, yeh that's it, look away now and I'll be right with you... Dammit, she's flown the coop again.

But no matter. I shall saunter myself over to the nearest wastepaper receptacle and have a good old rummage around the chip cartons, cardboard coffee cups and discarded Christmas cards to see what I can salvage before the long cold night sets in and then seek some refuge in whoever takes my fancy.

And what d'ya know? Lucky old Billy Goat Gruff here has struck lucky for once in his boy pigeon life. A full nine-inch rotting frankfurter, a packet of Golden Wonder and a small hip flask of lemon myrtle syrup. God only knows how that lot got here but who am I to wonder about the whys and wherefores. I've waited for this moment for years and shall waste no time gathering my finds under my substantial wingspan and shield them from those praying-mantis seagulls.

Cos mark my words, those gulls are evil bastards. They'll rip your throat out soon as squawk at you. And if they think for a second that you've struck lucky in the jetsam and flotsam of pigeon existence, they're all over you, beating their wings at you, stabbing and screeching in your pigeon face until you beg them to stop but it'll be no use unless you surrender your finds to them, no questions asked.

But not this time, no siree. Those fuckwit albatross bastard offspring ain't frightening me away from my gleaming stash of Rotting Frankfurter, Golden Wonder and Myrtle Syrup. If they think they can scare me away, then they've got another think coming to their razor sharp yellow spotted beaks. Cos this find is mine and I ain't sharing it with any gin swilling cigar smoking anchovy farting sea bird who's lost his way and is taking it out on some poor hapless boy pigeon who's only trying to plot his way through his inconsequential life with the occasional assistance of a… Ooo steady on lady, there you go, just one minute... Dammit she's flown the coop again.

No, this time me and my collection of goodies are going somewhere safe and sound, free from the prying eyes of those thieving vultures and other lesser spotted vermin who take an unhealthy interest in my hard-fought collections. Somewhere they'll never guess in a trillion years. This way my lovelies, just come this way with your friendly old boy pigeon, steady now...

The Pigeon's Tale

MEET THE CREATIVE TEAM

S

We(are)Three Kings of Leyton Orient aren't we?

About the Writer: Nick Owen

Recipient of the MBE in 2012 for his outstanding contributions to arts-based businesses, Nick possesses an unwavering passion for fostering culturally enriching and socially engaging creative practices within educational settings, both on a national and international scale. With a diverse career spanning the creative and cultural industries, he has ventured into the realms of public, private, and social enterprise sectors in regions such as the East Midlands, Merseyside, and Cumbria.

He remains deeply committed to establishing global connections, cultivating partnerships in countries like Bulgaria, Chile, India, and Serbia, among others. Beyond his academic pursuits, he is an avid cyclist, a skilled tennis player, a talented fiction writer, and a proficient Vinyl DJ. His recent publications include:

- Tabloid!!! (with Gary Carpenter) (2024)
- A Spell in the Army (2024)
- Confessions off an Ageing Figure Skater (2024)
- Confessions of an Aspiring Basketball Player (2023)
- Confessions of an Ageing Football Player (2023)
- Confessions of an Ageing Tennis Player" (2021)
- No Such Thing as an Englishman (2020)
- Racing Trains (2018)
- Mess Theory (2017)

About the Illustrator: Paul Warren

Paul Warren has always sketched and drawn and painted images. In 2013, after renting studio space at Harrington Mill Studios in Long Eaton, he began drawing on an iPad and he has drawn on an iPad ever since. He calls his artwork, *Momentism*. A phrase he has coined is "the iPad is my sketch pad" and it fits very well. His drawing style is continually evolving and developing. He draws people, the human figure and adds a sprinkling of artistic license. He doesn't strictly create pictures; he's interested in facial expression, stance, form, interaction between members of society, a moment in the workaday activities.

About the Editor: Alexander Moore

Before becoming an editor and writer, Alexander Moore worked as an actor, performing in hundreds of theatrical shows throughout the UK and Europe. This naturally transitioned into roles creating and directing workshops and plays, before settling down and focusing on the written word.

He has edited over 50 books for children and young adults, and numerous academic manuscripts written by eminent scholars.

He has collaborated with writers of fiction, biographies, and screenplays, but also award-winning publishers, universities, charities, and regional businesses.

He has worked in Germany (good beer), Italy (good food), and Siberia (super cold!) and was a guest speaker at the University of Oslo. He has written and directed plays for young people and led many workshops about understanding Shakespeare's texts, script development, and modern social issues, like internet safety.

More details here: www.advancedediting.co.uk

Printed in Great Britain
by Amazon

51301344R00048